Hi Boys,

Grandpa Keith

loves you like a Big

Bear !! oo

God Bless !! oo

Keith

Written by Jillian Harker
Illustrated by Daniel Howarth

This is a Parragon Publishing book
First published in 2006

Parragon Publishing
Queen Street House
4 Queen Street
BATH BA1 1HE, UK

ISBN 1-40548-627-9
Printed in China

I Love You, Grandpa

p

Little Bear and Grandpa were walking
by the river when Little Bear spotted a fish
darting through the water.
"Quick, Grandpa!" he yelled.

He rushed into the river, caught the fish, and held it up proudly for Grandpa to see.

Grandpa smiled. "You're fast, Little Bear," he said. "I can remember when I was as fast as you."

He started to cross the river and turned to Little Bear.

"My legs were once strong and speedy like yours," he added. "But now I've found an easier way to catch a meal."

"Really, Grandpa?" asked Little Bear. "What's that?"

"Well," replied Grandpa, "I'm more crafty now." He stopped on a rock.

"I stand here at the rapids," Grandpa said, standing very still. "I'm patient. I wait until the fish jump out of the water… straight into my mouth."

"Wow!" said Little Bear.
"I love you, Grandpa.
You're so clever!"

Just then, Eagle swooped down.
The beat of his wings ruffled the bears'
fur. They saw his sharp claws.

Little Bear ran straight up a tree. Grandpa smiled.

"I can remember when I could climb as well as you," he said. "My arms were strong. But now I don't need to run away."

"Really, Grandpa?" asked Little Bear. "What do you do instead?"

"Well," replied Grandpa, "I'm bolder now." When Eagle swooped again, Grandpa barked in his deep, gruff voice. He roared, and Eagle swerved away over the mountains.

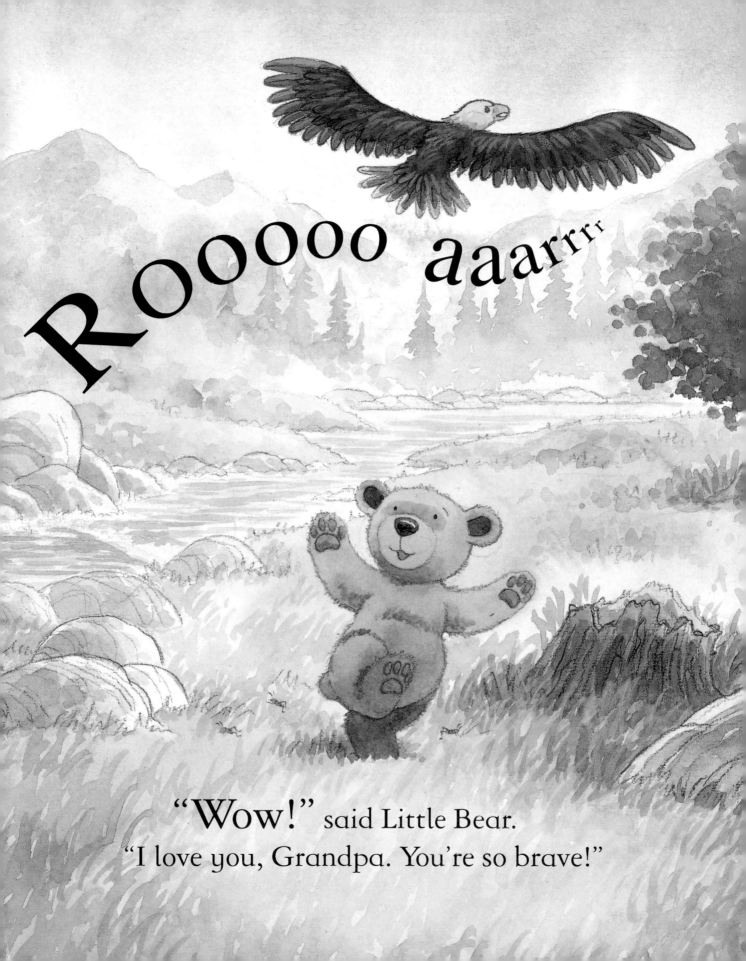

ROOOOO aaarrr

"Wow!" said Little Bear.
"I love you, Grandpa. You're so brave!"

They walked on until they came
across a slope, where the earth was softer
and deeper.

"Watch me, Grandpa!" called Little Bear.
"I can dig myself a really good hollow to
sleep in through the winter."
And Little Bear began to scrape away the soil.

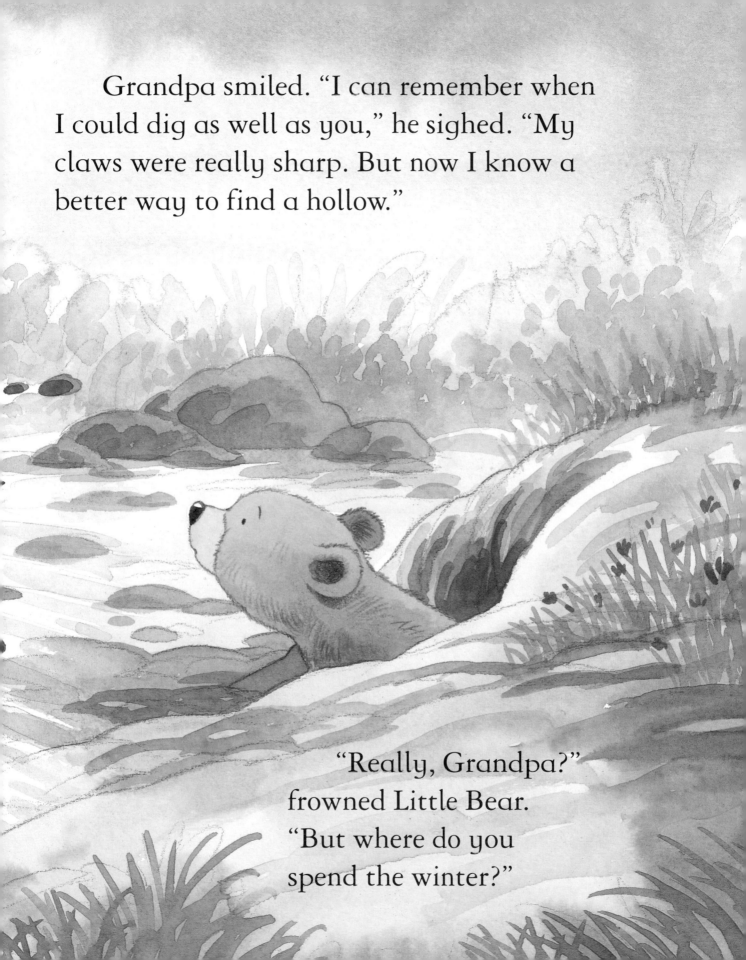

Grandpa smiled. "I can remember when I could dig as well as you," he sighed. "My claws were really sharp. But now I know a better way to find a hollow."

"Really, Grandpa?" frowned Little Bear. "But where do you spend the winter?"

"Well," replied Grandpa, "I'm wiser now.
All I need to do is to find a hollow tree."
He padded through the woods in front of
Little Bear. "Follow me," he called.
And he led Little Bear to a huge tree.

In the middle of its massive trunk was a snug hollow. "I love you, Grandpa," laughed Little Bear. "You know so much."

Little Bear looked up at Grandpa.
"Will I ever be as crafty, brave, and
wise as you?" he asked.

"Of course you will!" replied Grandpa.
"Shall I start teaching you now?"
Little Bear nodded.

So Grandpa took Little Bear to the rapids
and taught him the crafty way to catch a fish...

...and the brave way to scare a bird away.
Little Bear learned quickly.

Soon soft flakes of snow began to fall.

"It's time to find us a hollow tree big enough for two," Grandpa said.

And he helped Little Bear to choose wisely.

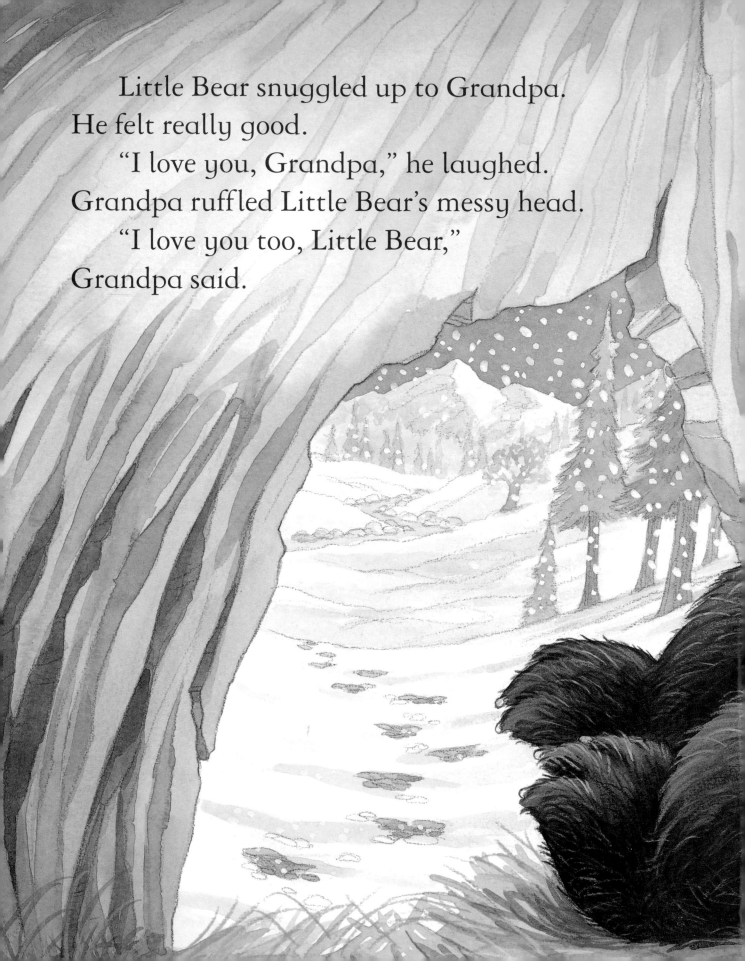

Little Bear snuggled up to Grandpa.
He felt really good.
   "I love you, Grandpa," he laughed.
Grandpa ruffled Little Bear's messy head.
   "I love you too, Little Bear,"
Grandpa said.